P9-CML-436

597.96 SNA

597.96
SNA
BC#36700065115183 $12.95
Snakes!

Snakes!

By the Editors of TIME FOR KIDS
WITH LISA JO RUDY

HarperCollins*Publishers*

About the Author: Lisa Jo Rudy writes about science, technology, history, and social studies for kids. She also helps to create exhibits, planetarium shows, hands-on kits, and educational materials. Lisa lives near Philadelphia, Pennsylvania, with her husband, two children, two fish, one cat, and zero snakes.

To Tommy, Sara, and of course my wonderful husband, Peter

Special thanks to Tanya Minott and the Philadelphia Zoo *–L.J.R.*

LIBRARY OF CONGRESS CATALOGING-IN-PUBLICATION DATA

Snakes! / by the editors of Time for Kids with Lisa Jo Rudy.— 1st ed.
p. cm. — (Time for kids science scoops)
ISBN 0-06-057636-7 (pbk.) — ISBN 0-06-057637-5 (trade)
1. Snakes—Juvenile literature. I. Rudy, Lisa Jo. II. Time for kids online.
III. Series.

QL666.06S665 2005 2004004323
597.96—dc22

5 6 7 8 9 10
First Edition

Photography and Illustration Credits:
Cover (green tree python): Gary McVicker—Index Stock; cover inset (banded mongoose): Paul Souders—Getty Images; cover front flap (natal green snake): Digital Vision; cover back flap (snake skin) Getty Images; title page (emerald tree boa): Marian Bacon—Animals Animals; contents page: (garter snake): Getty Images; pp. 4–5: R. Andrew Odum—Peter Arnold; pp. 6–7: Karen Beckhardt; p. 7 (inset): IT Stock Free/Picturequest; pp. 8–9: Michael Fogden—Bruce Coleman; p. 9 (inset, top): Erwin & Peggy Bauer—Bruce Coleman; p. 9 (inset, bottom): Fred Bavendam—Peter Arnold; pp. 10–11: Michael & Patricia Fogden—Minden; pp. 12–13: Joe McDonald—Visuals Unlimited; p. 13 (inset): Karen Beckhardt; pp. 14–15: Michael Fogden—Animals Animals; p. 14 (inset): R. J. Erwin—DRK Photo; pp. 16–17: Joe McDonald—DRK Photo; pp. 18–19: Joe McDonald—Animals Animals; p. 18 (inset, left): Wolfgang Bayer—Bruce Coleman; p. 18 (inset, center): Wolfgang Bayer—Bruce Coleman; p. 19 (inset): Erwin & Peggy Bauer—Bruce Coleman; pp. 20–21: Stephen Dalton—Photo Researchers; p. 21 (inset): Michael Fogden—DRK Photo; pp. 22–23: Digital Vision; p. 23 (inset): Michael & Patricia Fogden—Minden; pp. 24–25: Daniel Heuclin—Peter Arnold; pp. 26–27: Ed Reschke—Peter Arnold; p. 27 (inset): David A. Northcott—Corbis; pp. 28–29: G. C. Kelley—Photo Researchers; p. 29 (inset): William Leonard—DRK Photo; pp. 30–31: Cosmos Blank—NAS/Photo Researchers; p. 30 (inset): Greg O'Neill—Philadelphia Zoo; p. 32 (constrictor): Wolfgang Bayer—Bruce Coleman; p. 32 (dislocate): Stephen Dalton—Photo Researchers; p. 32 (fangs): Charles Schwartz—Animals Animals; p. 32 (keratin): G. C. Kelley—Photo Researchers; p. 32 (molt): Cosmos Blank—NAS/Photo Researchers; p. 32 (venom): Michael & Patricia Fogden—Minden; p. 32 (reticulated python): Joe McDonald—Visuals Unlimited; p. 32 (green anaconda): Rexford Lord—Photo Researchers; p. 32 (indian python): E. R. Degginger—Bruce Coleman; p. 32 (diamond python): Ken Stepnell—Bruce Coleman; back cover (emerald tree boa): Joe McDonald—Visuals Unlimited; back cover inset (corn snake): Getty Images

Acknowledgments:
For TIME FOR KIDS: Editorial Director: Keith Garton; Editor: Nelida Gonzalez Cutler; Art Director: Rachel Smith; Photography Editor: Jill Tatara

HarperCollins books may be purchased for educational, business, or sales promotional use. For information, please write: Special Markets Department, HarperCollins Publishers Inc., 10 East 53rd Street, New York, NY 10022.

CONTENTS

Garter snake

CHAPTER ONE

Snake Secrets

Emerald tree boa

Revealed

Something slithers through the forest. It moves silently, looking from side to side through lidless eyes. It is covered in brilliant green scales. It seems to disappear into the leaves. It's a snake!

shhhh...

Snakes are reptiles.

Crocodiles, alligators, turtles, and lizards are reptiles, too. All reptiles are cold-blooded. That means their blood stays the same temperature as the air around them. Here are the parts of a snake:

NO EARS: Snakes do not have ears or eardrums. They hear differently from humans. Bones in their heads vibrate when anything makes a noise.

EYES: Snake eyes are lidless. Most snakes see very well.

FANGS: Poisonous snakes keep their venom inside hollow, pointed fangs. Some snakes can fold their fangs back against the roofs of their mouths between bites.

TONGUE: Snakes use their tongues the way we use our noses. They "sniff" the air to check for enemies and food.

SKIN: Snakes are covered with smooth, clear scales. Snakes molt, or shed their skins, as they grow.

MUSCLES: Muscles along snakes' bodies help them to slither along.

SKELETON: All reptiles have backbones. Snakes have long backbones made up of at least one hundred smaller bones.

Snakes have no arms, legs, wings, or flippers.

They can't walk or run. So snakes move forward by tightening and relaxing their muscles.

Some snakes, such as vipers, boas, and pythons, keep their front and back ends on the ground. They raise their middles up high—much like inchworms.

Sidewinders fling their middles sideways to glide along quickly.

Sidewinder

The black mamba can slither from side to side up to seven miles an hour. It is the fastest snake in the world.

Sea snakes use their paddle-shaped tails to zip through the water.

CHAPTER TWO

Snakes Alive!

Bushmaster snakes come out of their shells.

Most snakes lay eggs. Forty or more eggs may hatch at one time! Some snakes lay eggs in nests and leave them to hatch on their own. Predators eat some of these eggs and baby snakes.

Reticulated python

Some snakes stay with their eggs and keep them warm.
It's tough to do, because snakes are cold-blooded. Mother pythons coil around their eggs and shiver. The shivering keeps

How Big?

The reticulated python is the longest snake in the world. It is found in Southeast Asia.

A small zoo in Indonesia claims it owns a python that is almost forty-nine feet long. That snake is as long as a tractor trailer! It weighs nine hundred ninety pounds.

Valley garter snakes are found thoughout North America.

Horned viper

Snakes live almost everywhere!

The only places where there are no snakes are Ireland, New Zealand, and the North and South Poles.

The horned viper lives in the North African desert. Its horns protect its eyes from the strong sun.

CHAPTER THREE

Hissing Hunters

hissssss...

Snakes are hunters. Some hiss loudly before they strike their prey. But most hide silently in water, trees, or burrows—and then attack.

The garden tree boa lives in the rain forests of Central and South America. When this boa senses its prey, it pounces!

Anacondas hide in shallow water.
When something tasty passes by, they grab it with their teeth. Then they drag it under the water. Anacondas are constrictors. They coil

their long bodies around their prey. Each time the captured animal takes a breath, the snake tightens its hold. The snake squeezes so tightly that its prey can't breathe.

A hungry anaconda grabs, strangles, and eats a meal. It swallows its prey whole.

Snakes shake, rattle, and roll!

Rattlesnakes' rattles are made of rings of keratin—the same material as your fingernails. The rings are attached to the end of the rattler's tail. A rattler gets a new ring each time it sheds its skin.

Rattlers shake their tails when they're scared. The rings knock together and make noise. Most animals run from the sound of this venomous snake!

A western diamondback rattlesnake gets ready to strike.

SUPER-SIZED SNAKE SNACKS!

Is a snake's mouth big enough to swallow an egg or an animal? Snakes can dislocate their jaws so that their mouths become huge. Even a small snake can eat a super-sized snack. It can take weeks for a snake to digest just one meal. The biggest snakes can eat whole pigs, monkeys, and deer.

RATTLE! RATTLE!

Fang-tastic!

Venomous snakes poison their prey. They use their fangs to inject venom when they bite. Spitting cobras also spray their venom. They can spit venom from their fangs at an enemy eight feet away!

Mozambique spitting cobra

A CURE FOR SNAKEBITE

Not all snakes bite, and not all biting snakes are venomous. But the venom from some snakes can make people sick. A bite from an adder, cobra, or rattler can kill!

Antivenom is a medicine that can cure snakebite. It's made in a lab from snake venom. Snakes are forced to bite through rubber stretched over a container. The venom that drips into the container is used to make the medicine. Doctors give it to snakebite victims.

A russell's viper gets milked for venom.

CHAPTER FOUR

What Scares Snakes?

Big cats, rats, hedgehogs, birds, and even some insects eat snakes and snake eggs. Many animals, such as mongooses, are immune to snake venom. That means they can eat venomous snakes without getting a stomachache!

The cobra's venom cannot harm this mongoose.

How do snakes stay safe?

Even snakes without venom have many ways to protect themselves. Most snakes quickly slither away when they sense danger. The ball python curls up and waits for its enemy to pass.

The hognose snake pretends to die. It flips over and lies on its back. Sometimes it even sticks out its tongue!

Hognose snake

Ball python

Some snakes can poop whenever they want. They make themselves so dirty and smelly that predators won't eat them. Yuck!

The western diamondback rattlesnake lives in Arizona, New Mexico, and Texas.

Snakes are in danger.

Humans are destroying snakes and their habitats. The western diamondback rattlesnake is endangered. It is hunted for its meat and skin.

Most snakes are not harmful to humans. They are important to the balance of nature. They keep the population of rats, mice, and birds under control.

DO PYTHONS MAKE GOOD PETS?

Some snakes make good pets. Corn snakes and garter snakes, such as this one, are beautiful, friendly, and easy to care for. Other snakes should be left alone. Some are endangered and many, including pythons, are dangerous.

Visit the Reptile House!

Tanya Minott is a zookeeper at the Reptile House at the Philadelphia Zoo in Pennsylvania. When she was eleven, she volunteered to care for injured animals at a museum. When she was fifteen, Minott started working summers at the Children's Zoo, which is part of the Philadelphia Zoo. Now she works with snakes and lizards. She feeds them and cleans their cages. She also teaches visitors about these reptiles.

"There's no reason to be scared of snakes," says Minott. But she admits that it is a challenge to keep snakes happy—and in their cages. "They are extremely good escape artists," she says. "If they find an opening, they use it!"

A garter snake sheds its skin.

Did You Know?

- Some snakes, such as vipers, boa constrictors, and pythons, can go as long as six months between meals.
- Female snakes are generally bigger than male snakes.
- Snakes molt at least once a year.
- Pit vipers can see heat. Their special heat-sensing "pits" help them find prey at night.
- In India, snake charmers play their flutes to make cobras dance. But snakes can't hear high-pitched sounds. Instead, the snakes are swaying along with the movement of the flute.

WORDS to Know

Constrictor: a type of snake that tightens its coils to suffocate its prey

Keratin the material that rattlesnal rattles are made from

Dislocate: to unhinge; a snake has the ability to unhinge its jaws so that it can eat large prey

Molt: to shed skin

Fangs: long, sharp teeth used for injecting venom

Venom: the poison in snakes' fang

FUN FACTS TOP 5 LONGEST SNAKE

1 **Reticulated Python** Average length: 35 feet

2 **Green Anaconda** Average length: 28 feet

3 **Indian Python** Average length: 25 feet

4 **Diamond Python** Average length: 21 feet

5 **King Cobra** Average length: 19 feet